W9-BGW-069

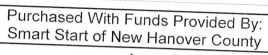

Smart Start Growing Readers

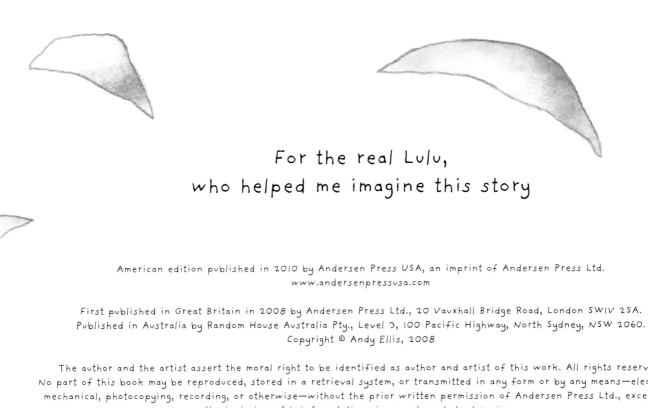

For the real Lulu,
who helped me imagine this story

American edition published in 2010 by Andersen Press USA, an imprint of Andersen Press Ltd.
www.andersenpressusa.com

First published in Great Britain in 2008 by Andersen Press Ltd., 20 Vauxhall Bridge Road, London SW1V 2SA.
Published in Australia by Random House Australia Pty., Level 3, 100 Pacific Highway, North Sydney, NSW 2060.
Copyright © Andy Ellis, 2008

Distributed in the United States and Canada by
Lerner Publishing Group, Inc.
241 First Avenue North
Minneapolis, MN 55401 U.S.A.
www.lernerbooks.com

Library of Congress Cataloging-in-Publication Data Available.
ISBN: 978-0-7613-5499-4

Printed and bound in Singapore.
1 — TWP — 9/10/09
This book has been printed on acid-free paper.

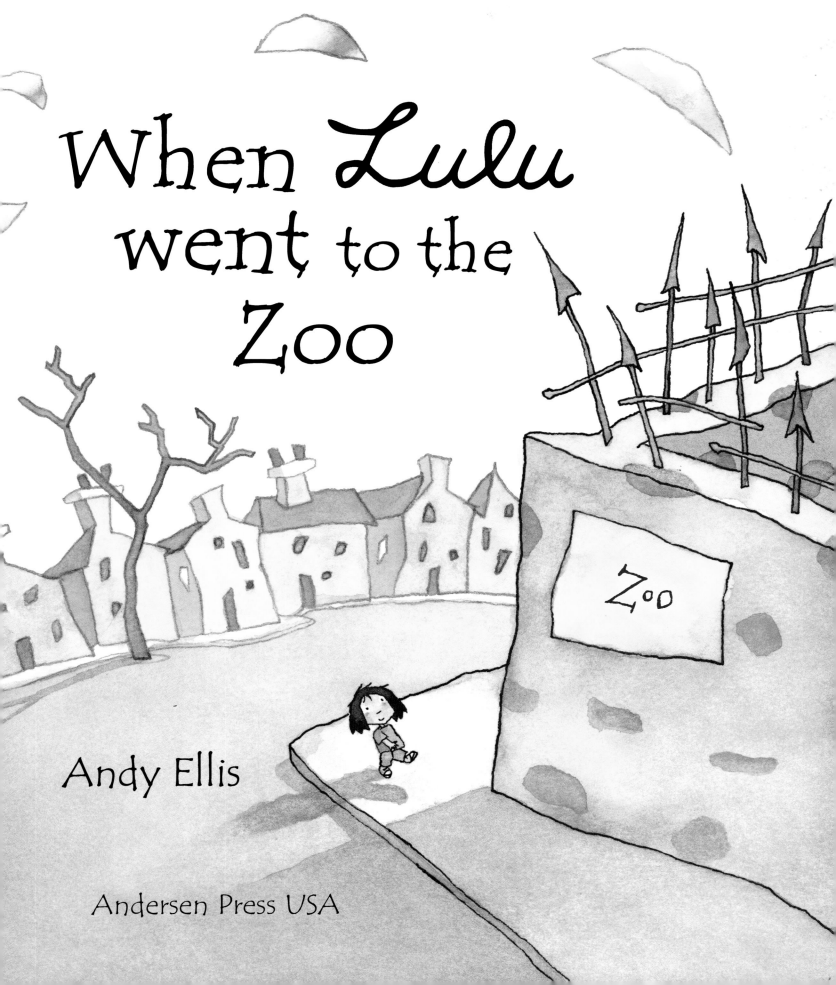

When Lulu went to the Zoo

Andy Ellis

Andersen Press USA

When Lulu went to the zoo . . .

she was sad for the giraffes
and the penguins too.

The tigers were crying really big tears
and the life had gone out of the llamas' ears.

Though Lulu was only two times two,
she knew that animals should not be in a zoo.

And though Lulu was the size
that Lulu should be,

she found that she might
(though it was a bit tight)

fit through the bars
of the cages with ease

and chat with the animals
as she swung through the trees.

She had to be careful
so nobody saw.
Then she slipped out again
through the little cage door.

And what she discovered,
while she talked to them all,

was they dreamed of splashing in a real waterfall.
Or dancing on icebergs that filled up the sea.

Or flying in the sky, flamingo or bee.

In short, to know how it feels to be free.

She whispered to the animals,
"You can come to my house.
There's room for you all,
from elephant to mouse."

And one moonless night she let them all go
and smuggled them back so no one would know.

And they lived with sweet Lulu
in sweet Lulu's house.

But there wasn't **quite** room for elephant and mouse.

The fridge was too full of penguins and seals.
There was no room for food, so no one had meals.

And the bathroom was the right place
for a lovely hot wash.

But the bear in the bathtub
was a bit of a squash.

Though Lulu loved them with a love very deep, it was never an easy secret to keep.

"We've found you!"
the six sad zookeepers said.
"Please give back our animals,
we'll put them to bed."

But Lulu was bold and she said, "Don't you see?
The zoo's not the place for my best friends to be.
Everyone of them says they just want to be free."

And she talked,
as only a four-year-old can,
of an idea she had
that was called Lululand.

Lulu and the zookeepers
imagined a place
where each of the animals
had oodles of space.

Now whenever she wants to
she tiptoes away,
to visit her friends and play there all day...

Welcome to
Lululand!

... but on warm, moonlit nights
she invites them all back,
when no one is looking,

for a BIG midnight snack!